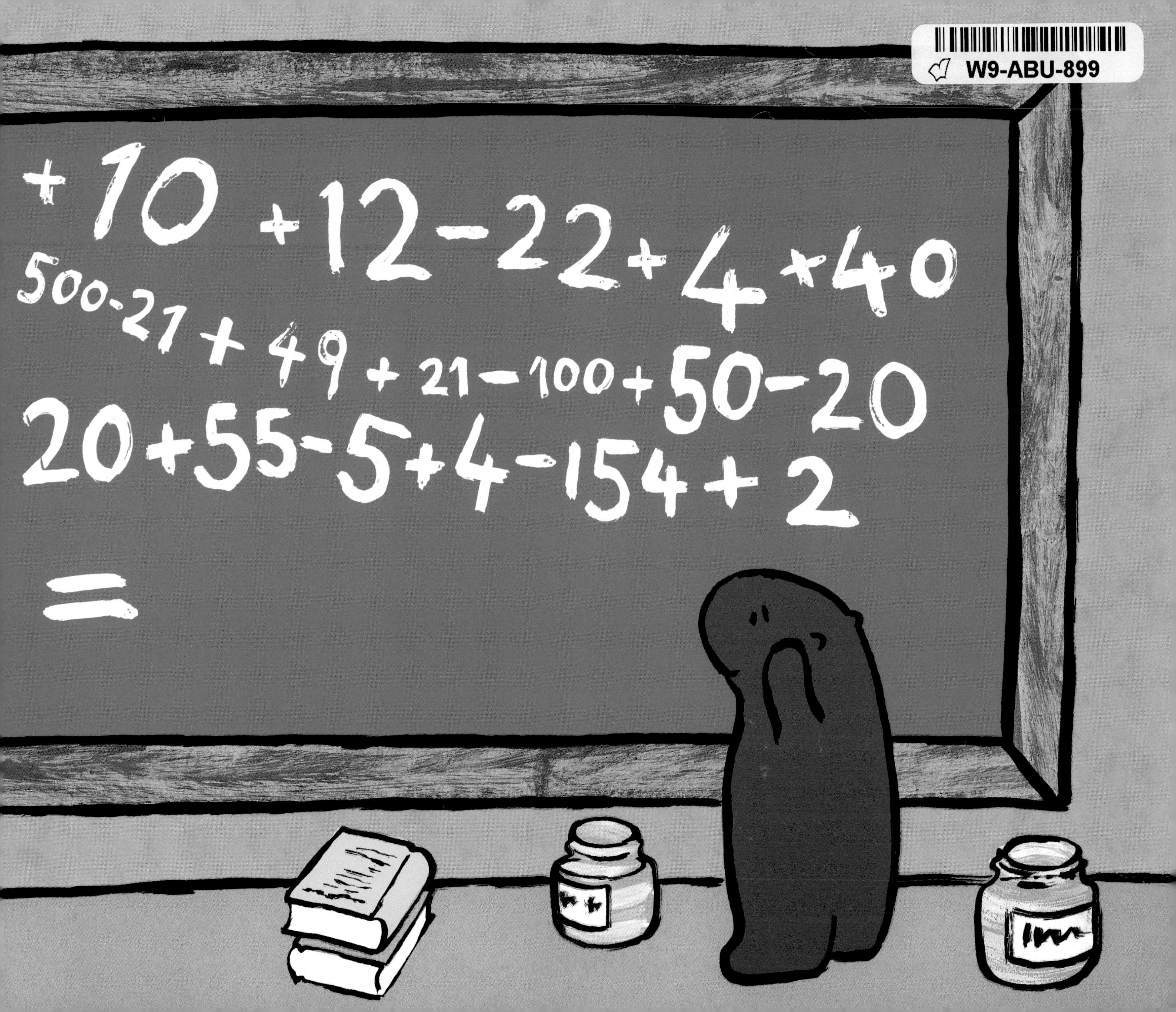
+10 +12-22+4+40
500-21+49+21-100+50-20
20+55-5+4-154+2
=

For Sarah, who
introduced me
to Eric

THIS IS A BORZOI BOOK PUBLISHED BY ALFRED A. KNOPF

Copyright © 2003 Caroline Glicksman

All rights reserved under International and Pan-American Copyright Conventions.
Published in the United States by Alfred A. Knopf, an imprint of Random House
Children's Books, a division of Random House, Inc., New York, and
simultaneously in Canada by Random House of Canada Limited,
Toronto. Distributed by Random House, Inc., New York.
Originally published in Great Britain in 2003 as *Eric the Red* by
The Bodley Head, an imprint of Random House Children's Books.
KNOPF, BORZOI BOOKS, and the colophon are registered
trademarks of Random House, Inc.

Library of Congress Cataloging-in-
Publication Data
Glicksman, Caroline.
Eric the math bear / Caroline Glicksman.
p. cm.
Summary: Eric the bear is unusually good at math, and when
robbers try to steal the money at the bank, he uses his
numerical skill to save the day.
[1. Bears—Fiction. 2. Mathematics—Fiction.] I. Title.
PZ7.G48845 Er 2003
[E]—dc21   2002073094
ISBN 0-375-82432-4 (trade)
ISBN 0-375-92432-9 (lib. bdg.)

www.randomhouse.com/kids
Printed in Malaysia
August 2003
10 9 8 7 6 5 4 3 2 1
First American Edition

Eric the Math Bear

Caroline Glicksman

Alfred A. Knopf

New York

Eric is a very
unusual bear.

Most bears are
brown or black
or white.

BATBEAR
BEAR WORLD 1
DEN DECOR
BEAR WORLD 4
SUPERBEAR
GRIZZLY MYSTERIES
BATBEAR 5
MORE GRIZZLY MYSTERIES
THE PICNIC
BEAR WORLD 7
GREAT BEARS IN HISTORY 15

BEAR WORLD

BEAR WORLD 2

PANDA PLANET

BEAR WORLD 3

For one thing,
Eric is red.

HONEY
SPECIAL RESERVE

Very red.

So red that he glows
in the dark.

And Eric is very, very clever, especially with numbers.

He even dreams
about numbers!

Eric likes counting things on his way to work.

This morning he saw:

two yellow trucks

four bears fishing

six red cars

eight boats on the river

Eric has a very important job at the Big Bear Bank.

Every day, he counts up
all the bank's money and
puts it in the big safe.

Then he thinks up a
new set of numbers for
the lock and closes
the safe tight.

Eric is the only bear
who knows the numbers!

Every so often, Eric helps
at the front counter of the bank.
He doesn't like working
there because
sometimes badly
behaved bears laugh
at his red fur.

He glows!

Heh! Heh!

THIS WAY

I'm in
the bank.

Then Eric wishes
he were at home,
eating lots of
honey and doing
bigger and bigger
sums on his computer.

But today the first customer had such kind, friendly eyes that Eric didn't mind.

"My name is Erica," she said. "I'd like to start saving—"

MORE MATH

POLAR ICES

POLAR ICES

POLAR ICES

THIS WAY

VROOM!

Just then an ice cream truck
burst through the door of the
bank and two polar bears
jumped out. Erica gasped.

"EVERYONE FREEZE!"

shouted the first polar bear. He gave Eric a note.

It said:

GIV US ALL
the MUNNy
NOW

Eric didn't like being told
what to do.

Without thinking, he growled at the first polar bear.

The polar bear was so surprised that he stepped back, slipped on an ice pop, and banged his head on the floor.

In a flash, the second polar bear grabbed Erica, jumped over the glass screen, and spun Eric around on his chair. Fast.

"TELL ME THE NUMBERS TO OPEN THE SAFE, TOMATO FACE!" he shouted.

"OR I'LL EAT THIS LITTLE BEAR FOR A SNACK!"

Eric's head spun. Millions of numbers whirled around in his head. How would he remember the ones he needed to save Erica?

"YOU'VE GOT FIVE SECONDS!" shouted the polar bear.

"FIVE!

FOUR!!

THREE!!!

TWO!!!!"

MORE MATH

"Wait!" gasped Eric. "That's it! TWO! The two-times table! The numbers of things I saw this morning. Two . . . four . . ."

The polar bear dropped Erica and started turning the lock on the safe.

"Six . . . eight . . . ten . . . ," continued Eric, but his head was spinning so much that he couldn't remember the last number.

"TWELVE . . . ," said Erica. Suddenly, the safe opened and the polar bear started grabbing the money as fast as he could. Soon he was right inside the safe.

Eric's head stopped spinning.

LOOT

He helped Erica to her feet and . . .

Wah! Wah! Wah!

Five police bears rushed in and arrested the first polar bear, who was still lying dazed on the floor.

"You caught them red-handed!" said Erica. She gave Eric's paw a gentle squeeze.

"I couldn't have done it alone," said Eric. Suddenly, he noticed . . .

. . . the math book that Erica
was holding in her paws.
"You like math too!" he said.

"I've never met another bear
who liked numbers," said Erica.

Eric glowed very red.

"Wouldn't it be fun to do sums
together?" said Erica.

Eric grinned. "Yes, twice as
much fun!" he said.

$$1 + 1 + 2 + 4 + 6 + 8$$
$$+ 34 + 100 - 20 + 5 + 16 + 4 + 16 +$$
$$+ 5 - 55 + 2 + 48 - 520 +$$
$$- 42 + 2 - 60$$